Printed and bound in Singapore

Library of Congress Cataloging-in-Publication Data
Rock, Lois, 1953-
  When goodbye is forever / Lois Rock ; illustrated by Sheila Moxley.
    p. cm.
  ISBN 1-56148-449-0 (hardcover)
1. Bereavement--Religious aspects--Juvenile literature. 2. Death--Religious aspects--Juvenile
literature. 3. Future life--Juvenile literature. I. Moxley, Sheila. II. Title.
  BL65.B47R63 2004
  242'.4--dc22   2004007827

When Good-Bye Is Forever

Lois Rock
Illustrated by Sheila Moxley

Intercourse, PA 17534
800/762-7171
www.goodbks.com

From the time you were small,
you have learned to say good-bye.

These are little good-byes
for a short time
when you aren't together.

There are longer good-byes.
Sometimes you know how long
they will last.

Sometimes you don't.

Some good-byes are forever.

These good-byes may be happy.

For in every ending there is also
a beginning, and some good-byes
feel like happy new beginnings
and bright days.

Some good-byes that are forever may be sad.

They can make you feel lost and lonely.

You may want to cry.

You may want someone to hug you and to comfort you until the pain and sadness go away.

So when you have to say good-bye
forever to someone you love,
that is the saddest good-bye of all.

But people do die.

Just as the flowers die,
just as the leaves die,
just as little creatures die.

In the end, everyone must die.

Sometimes death comes
unexpectedly, like a frost
that kills the spring flowers.

It seems so unkind, so unfair.

Sometimes death is expected,
just as winter follows autumn.

When someone you love has died, you may feel sadder and lonelier than ever before.

It may seem that you will cry forever.

It may seem that the pain and sadness will never go away.

It may seem that no one can love you enough to help you.

Time will pass.

Into the empty space of good-bye will come the memories of happy times.

Just as morning follows night and spring follows winter, there will be new beginnings: new people to meet, new things to do.

Loved ones who die
pass on to a new beginning.
They go to a new place that is
beyond what we can see, beyond
what we can fully understand.

We call that place heaven,
where God makes all things new;
where those we love are safe
in the love of God, as we are
safe in the love of God.

They will be out of sight
for only a little time,
for God's love will gather us
together for all eternity.